HIS PROMISED GIFT

HIS
PROMISED
GIFT

CHRISTINA STOKESBURY

His Promised Gift
by Christina Stokesbury

Copyright © 2020 Christina Stokesbury

Title Inspiration: Shaun Dillehay
Editors: Annette Deckard and Kara Starcher
Cover Design: Funnel Design Group
Cover Approval: Sean Cobb
Cover Artist: Madeline Hancock
Interior Layout: Kara Starcher

ISBN: 978-0-578-76930-3
Library of Congress Control Number: 2020917631

31 30 29 28 27 26 25 24 23 22   2 3 4 5 6

*To all the mothers and fathers who have lost big,
to all the families who have been through a tragic accident,
and to all who are dealing with loss —*

*You are not alone during your journey
of grief, healing, and pain.
God knows your pain.
He knows there is more than
what our natural eyes see here on earth.*

*No matter the depths of your pain,
God loves you.
He is with you during all seasons of your life.*

Blessings, freedom, and love to all who read.

CONTENTS

This book is fiction,
but even with fiction,
much that is said is true.

AUTHOR'S NOTE

I believe it's truly important for my readers to know why I write and where my heart is at when I write a new book. Each book is written to help others.

My inspiration for this fiction story was to help mothers, fathers, and families who have lost a child or loved one, to help them know that someone understands and can relate to such a traumatic experience, and to create an awareness that others have been through a similar life-altering event. That awareness tells us that, no matter our pain, we can still hope and a love is out there bigger than anything we could ever understand.

I know during my own loss of my child, nobody could get through to me. It didn't matter how many times I heard "he's in a better place," it never resonated, and instead of helping, that phrase always hurt and angered me. Now I write about loss because I know firsthand the feelings and emotions I went through during that time. I can't say I know and understand exactly what others have gone through during their own journey, because everyone heals, grieves, and processes feelings and pain differently. However, I can say that through my own experiences, my pathway through healing and my many years of processing the pain and heartache of that loss, I do know my son was raised by a loving Father in heaven. I also know that the devil comes to kill, steal, and destroy. I don't believe that God wants His people to go through pain, but it happens, and because it happens, we have to know that God is there with us every step of the way—even when we are angry and feel as if God has left us. He has never left us and never will. We just have to call on Him and remember His promises.

God understands our pain because He has been there with his own Son. He also knows there is life—a good life—beyond this realm we live in. So, as we go through our own journey in life, we need to always remember that gift God gave us before we were ever brought into this world. That gift is His son, and we need to continue to hold tight to His promises.

"And we know that in all things God works for the good of those who love him, who have been called according to his purpose."—Romans 8:28 (NIV)

I hope you enjoy this book.

Christina Stokesbury

CHAPTER 1

THE WIND

Have you ever found yourself just wondering what's next? Questioning life? Feeling like there has to be more? Or questioning heaven, faith, yourself, and even God? I found myself in this position of questioning everything in my life one evening back in 2017—a night I will always remember.

The sky had turned pink from the beautiful sunset as I sat on the front porch drinking my coffee and swinging calmly and slowly on my comfortably cushioned porch swing. I was still sore from the birth of my youngest son, and I was tired. The baby monitor rested on the table next to me, and I listened to the whirr of the baby's fan over the monitor. I'm not sure if the doubts and questions started because of postpartum depression or not, but I didn't feel like I had the "baby blues." I really think it was more of just being in a questioning phase of my life. You know, questioning life in general and wondering about heaven and if it existed.

You have to realize that for me to question heaven is a big deal. I was raised to never question God or heaven. But thinking about this more caused me to wonder—what have I seen, read, and heard that would persuade me to believe there was a heaven? And, more importantly, does God really love me? I had experienced many miracles in my life, so I've never questioned *if* there is a God. But now I reached a point in life where I just wanted to feel God's love and I wanted to seriously and wholeheartedly experience Him.

I was tired of living what felt like a mundane life. I didn't want to die, but I felt like giving up, so I decided it would be okay if God took me out of this world. I knew my kids would be okay with my awesome husband. I was simply ready to go live in heaven and see all of heaven's beauty and my mom. Oh, how I wanted to see and hug my mom again. I missed her so much.

I know how awful it sounds that I wanted to leave this world for heaven, but I'm sure people feel this way and just aren't willing to admit it. Not that one wants to die, but it's just that feeling of wanting more. More in life. Wanting to be more or to have something amazing happen that truly changes the winds of time. I was there, at that place. I wanted more. I wanted to be more than what I felt I had become or had lived. I had a great family. It wasn't them.

If I had to be here on earth, I wanted to be better. I

wanted to be a better mom, a better wife, a better everything. Not that I wasn't a good mom or wife, but I wanted to be that mom you saw in movies that made the lunches every morning for her kids. The mom who knew how to cook gourmet meals and who never raised her voice when someone wasn't listening. The mom who was relaxed even when everything felt like it was falling apart. I wanted to be that wife who gave her husband massages without complaining that she never got one. A wife who kept the laundry done and did the grocery shopping without buying snacks instead of real food (as my husband calls it). There were so many things I would change about myself and was ready to change but wasn't sure how much effort I could exert because I was also at that point of just throwing my hands up and saying "Okay, God, take me."

I guess I needed to figure it out. Figure me out. I needed to find myself. Actually, more than finding myself, I needed to find God and feel God's love again. Life had gotten so crazy with all the hustle and bustle of family life. I was in a whirlwind of chaos. That's really the best description of how I felt at that time.

Sometimes I look back at that night sitting on the porch and wonder if that night was what put everything into motion. Was there a wind that carried my thoughts to the heavens? Was that what caused the change in my life? Did God hear my questions? Did God see that I was going through some sort of spiritual quandary that God felt He needed to remove me from? My story after that night has many pieces in its puzzle of brokenness, but no matter what, I knew God was creating a beautiful life for me once my puzzle was complete.

Shortly after my night of questioning, everything in my life changed. My world turned upside down, and everything I believed, and was raised to know of God and heaven, was proven to be true.

How can I say heaven is true? I saw it for myself. I visited heaven. If it were my choice, I would have stayed there. I even begged God to let me stay, but He sent me back for a purpose. I wasn't happy that He sent me back, but I now understand why. It took time for me to see the reason, but as I tell you my story, you will see, as well, that there was a purpose. God had a plan for my family and me. He had a reason for my existence. All of the brokenness, the hurt, and the pain fell into place and created a story that could have stayed broken but instead was made beautiful in only a way God can design it.

I will never forget the day I visited heaven, mainly because I lost a part of my heart that day, but also because that was the day that changed my life forever. Before I go into detail about what happened to get me there, I first need to tell you a little bit about my family and my life prior to my heavenly visit.

Who I Am

I am a mom of five beautiful children. Now, I'm going to stop right here because I know what you must be thinking—how could you feel like giving up when you have five amazing kiddos? Like I said, it wasn't that I really wanted to give up; I just wanted to be more, to be better, and I needed to feel more in my life. And somehow, giving up seemed like the thing to do. I know that sounds crazy, but I'm speaking straight from my heart.

With five children, life can get busy and be nonstop. As a mom, I was always doing something or on the go. We were involved in everything—church, sports, moms' group, weekend family adventures, and more. That was my life.

My oldest boy is twenty years old. He left for college last year, and that was very hard on this momma. His name is John, and we had always been very close. The day he left for college had me in tears and wondering if I had taught him everything he needed to know to help him progress and be successful in life along with keeping him safe on his new journey. I wondered if he was going to make mistakes as many do when they go off to their first year of college or if he would hold to his biblical teachings and make good choices. All of the normal thoughts of "was I good enough as a mother" weighed heavily on me when he moved out of the house. However, I came to terms with the fact that I have to trust God and let John make mistakes and figure out life on his own. I had to let go of my first-born and let him grow into the adult he was becoming. My job shifted to continually praying over and for him.

My second oldest is a son named Mark. He was nine the day God took me to heaven. He is in fourth grade and loving school. He is outgoing and cute as can be. But I say that about all our children! Of course, as their mom, I think they are all the best and cutest, as any mom would. I have to say that all the girls love Mark with his outgoing personality and blond hair and blue eyes.

Our third child is also a boy, and his name is David. David turned seven years old the day I left this earth, the day that changed his world and our lives forever. He is our shy little guy. He isn't built as thick as Mark, but Mark looks more like a football player. David is big into playing the piano and is very artistic. He is quiet and smart and a complete introvert. His shyness is very becoming, but because he is so shy, he doesn't have a lot of friends. He considers staying home a thrill over going outside and playing. Sometimes, it's almost like pulling teeth to get him to leave the house.

Our fourth born is our only daughter. Her name is Esther. She is our wild child and a beauty with blond curly hair and blue eyes. She has a glow about her that is almost like a peaceful beautiful aura that covers her. This little girl loves with all that she has and forgives like we all should forgive. She has a heart for God and that makes this Momma proud. She was only four years old the day I left. She might not ever remember that day, and that's okay with me. I would rather her not go through life with a tragedy weighing on her shoulders. However, there are many things she will be told about that day.

Our youngest born is Elijah, our sweet baby boy who was only one month old the day my world stood still. He has more of a brown tint to his hair and skin, but he has blue eyes like the rest of his brothers and sister. He doesn't look like the rest of us so the hubs jokes around a lot calling him the milk man's baby. I know he is joking, but I do see that this little guy has different features than the rest of his siblings, and yet for some reason, I have always felt he would be the tallest and most outgoing of them all. Right now, he is a chillaxed baby and that is awesome! I guess God knew that I needed to have a baby that was calm after having Esther who keeps me on my toes constantly.

As you can see, all my children have biblical names. Yes, I am a Christian if you haven't figured that out already. I am a firm believer in Jesus, and I have been a Christian all my life. I am usually not one to straight out say "Christian" because I believe there is more to being a Christian than just announcing it. Being a Christian isn't a word or a claim. Being a Christian is about having a relationship with God. That is what I was raised to have—a complete and powerful relationship with God.

My relationship with God is probably why I was having doubt and questions the night the wind took my thoughts up to the heavens. I hadn't been consistently and fervently praying. I felt so far from God. And that is a bad feeling to have, especially when all you knew growing up was God and how you were to build a relationship with Him.

Because of how I was taught growing up, I believed I was always blessed. I felt it wasn't because of who I was but because of my mom and how close she herself was to God. God knew her, and still does, on a close relationship level.

My mom was an awesome single mother who raised me and my brother. She was a powerful believer in God. When she was young, she was raised to know God but not on the level that God brought her to know Him. She was a God-fearing, awesome woman who fully trusted Him. I always looked up to her. When I was growing up, she took us to church, which, quite honestly, was something I never looked forward to. Maybe it was because our church was full of old people and my being young meant I never had another kid to play or talk with.

Yes, I had an older brother, but we never really had that connection like other siblings. We were close, but we didn't play, fight, or even talk much at all. I do remember the few times we did hang out, and those were amazing, but after that, I don't remember much of him being around. It could be because he was so much older than me and he had other things that were more exciting to him than just hanging out with his little sister.

Even though my brother and I were never really like other brothers and sisters, we still helped each other occasionally with things like sports and practicing basketball together. We didn't fight like you see most siblings do; in fact, now that I have my own children and see how they love to irritate each other, I realize how odd my relationship with my brother really was. Looking back, maybe we were that way because our personalities were so different. I was the one who learned (through life lessons) very quickly.

I remember one time I decided I wanted my brother's attention so I did my best to bug him while he was studying. I started saying his name over and over and over again to get a rise out of him. He kept telling me to stop because he was studying. Of course, studying, in my mind, was silly. But not to him. The more I said his name, the more flustered he got with me until the moment he took off after me. He chased me all the way to my mom's room where I locked myself in (only because my mom wasn't home at the time). However, while he was chasing me, he accidentally stabbed his leg with the freshly sharpened pencil that he had been using for homework. So, the lessons I learned that day...One, don't run with a pencil because that looked very painful; and two, don't ever irritate your brother to the point of no return again. I feared for my life that day. Or at least for my arm that I knew was going to get a beating from him. My brother always had a calm demeanor, but when pushed, he wasn't so calm. So that was the only time I ever thought about or tried to irritate him. Because I wasn't an annoying, attention-grabbing younger sibling (at least not after that incident!), I figure that could be why we never really fought and we got along so well.

Another thing I noticed about my brother was that when he had a girlfriend that girl would be all that mattered in his life. And he carried that trait into adulthood when he got married, which of course was to be expected. He always had a one-track mind that didn't multitask well. Nothing against him because he is and has always been crazy smart. Plus, he always did everything right. (I was more the black sheep of the family.) But I will say he was a good brother who went to all my sporting events up until his graduation and he always rooted for me as I did for him as well.

Growing up we never really saw our dad, but our mom played a pretty awesome role as both parents. At least she did the best she could. Later in life, I did get to know my dad. He turned out to be a pretty cool guy, and I will tell you that I do see the many things I missed in life by not having him around. I also see God's plan in everything and how it all worked out.

My dad now comes around quite often to pick up Esther. He and Esther have a pretty strong bond that I am glad she has with him. She is still young, but she loves her grandpa and she gets so excited to see him when he visits. I love seeing them together; it's like the healing that I needed. God granted both Dad and me healing from our missed past together. However, like all things, God plans and works things out for our own well-being. I know God is still healing Dad from the guilt of not being around, and the Lord does know that I hold nothing against my dad for that. I know it was a different time in his life. He had a lot going on and needed a lot of healing before he could be brought back into our lives.

I love how my dad's wife and Mark, my nine-year-old, adore each other. Mark and Grandma are like best friends. They love each other and share everything. Grandma taught Mark how to ride a horse, a passion they now share together. Every couple of weeks, Grandma and Grandpa pick up both Esther and Mark, and sometimes their seven-year-old brother David, for a visit to their house. Even though I love my children with all that I have, it's always nice for a little break. When the three go to visit Grandma, this gives the hubs and me a little quiet time. However, we do still have Elijah at home, but with him being a newborn, he sleeps a lot so that helps me get revived.

My amazing husband Tom and I have been married for

twenty-three years last month. I never thought I would get married to a man in uniform because of past experiences, but I did, and I am glad I did. My husband is my true blessing. He is my "gift." He is everything I had wished for in a man, and God knew exactly what I needed.

I have to say, being raised without a dad and not knowing how kids really interact with a male figure, I have had fun these last twenty years watching Tom raise the children. Watching him (as a father) interact with the kids and teach them has helped me realize it's a totally different role than a mother's. And I have had to release a lot of the feeling of needing to do it all on my own because that is what I knew being raised by a single mother.

Tom is great with the kids, and he has a different bond with each one. Now, I know parents aren't supposed to have favorites, but I do see a more defined bond between Tom and David, our seven-year-old. I am not sure if it's because he is more like Tom or if it's because Tom feels sorry for him. I couldn't tell you why, but David is our shy little guy. He is sweet, innocent, and very loving. David also has a big connection to my husband's parents, Gammy and G-Pa. Even with David being a homebody, he will never say no to going to their house. He and his G-Pa will play pool for hours. He even enjoys going to Gammy's room and lying in bed with her to snuggle. Gammy has to lay down a lot when bad weather is around due to her joints and David knows this, so he takes it upon himself to go spend time with Gammy on those days. He isn't like most children that will look to his own playtime. He cares deeply about others and their feelings and it shows in everything he does.

I can't say I have always been the best mom because I know I have made plenty of mistakes. Like when Mark (my second oldest) was born, I felt like I was starting all over since it had been eleven years since my last child. Needless to say, Mark was extra spoiled. I feel John, my oldest, lost a lot of my attention, and for that, I have felt awful, but I didn't even realize my mistake until he moved out. The day John left for college, I felt a rain of feelings just drown me, and I started beating myself up about all the mistakes I had made as a mother while raising him. I have questioned myself and wondered what I could have done differently to help him become the man God has called him to be. I keep reminding myself that he knows his Momma loves him, and even though a lot of attention was taken away from him when Mark was born, it was only because the baby needed more attention to survive and not because we loved him any less. However, this is something I do regret as a mom, and I wish I could have done better when raising my sweet John.

I have to say that life has been good for our big family. I never dreamed I would have this many kids. And I would never complain because I was raised knowing that children are gifts from God and God must really trust me to give me such great gifts. I also know that with great love comes great responsibility, meaning taking care of these precious gifts.

CHAPTER 2

LOOKING BACK

I have always been known as a "sweet" person who loves her children with all she has. I wouldn't say that I am a saint by any means because I am far from it, but I do try hard to live a good life and to teach my children right from wrong. I strive to keep a good attitude and not talk badly about anyone. I truly believe that you reap what you sow, meaning you better sow good seeds for good to come back to you. I have also been told I wear humility beautifully; however, I am not sure if that is a compliment or not. I have always prayed that I would have a humble heart, so I am glad others feel I do, and maybe that means God sees a humble heart within me too.

Like most parents, I know of times that I have given into my kids just to get them to quit bugging me. I know that isn't great parenting, but yes, I am human, and I have made plenty of mistakes, and I am not too proud to admit it. However, my parenting skills aren't like others. I would say I have always been the overprotective parent who wouldn't even let my nine year old go play out front without an adult. Now, my husband Tom would let Mark roam the neighborhood with his friends when I wasn't home. The day I found out that was going on was the last day that ever happened. Of course, Mark got mad at me for not letting him go out and play while my husband made fun of me and asked the question of when I would ever let the kids grow up.

I just remember when I was sixteen, out for a jog in my neighborhood, and a car started following me. When I was on a street close to my home, I ran to a neighbor's house for safety and called the police. That day haunted me, and with everything in the world getting even worse, it always scares me to think of what could happen to any child playing outside without adult supervision. That is the part of me that lives in fear and creates the overprotection mode within myself.

When would I let them grow up? If I could hover over them until they graduated, I would be okay with that. I definitely want to make sure my children are safe from anyone who could harm or try to take them.

One thing I taught my kids very well is to stay away from scary-looking vans. I know that sounds funny, but that was something my mom always taught me. One time my kids and I were walking back from the school bus when I spotted a van parked on our street. I could see the driver just watching us walk home. I told my kids to go into the house, and once we were inside, we locked the doors. David, my shy, quiet son, grabbed Mark's bat and sat at the front window ready to jump into action and protect everyone if needed. He sat there for a while watching for strangers. Mark went and played upstairs like nothing happened. I felt bad that my son felt the need to sit there instead of playing, but he wasn't moving from that spot.

My husband said I am raising the kids to be paranoid, but my goal is to teach them to be aware of their surroundings. Awareness is something that needs to be taught to everyone, not just kids. We live in a dark world full of crazies. My goal is to keep that craziness as far away from my family as possible. I also know that bad things do happen even to good people. It's awful but true. However, I know that God holds our future in His hands, and I need to leave all of my worries and fears in His hands too.

In all actuality, worrying gets you nowhere in life. My husband always says worrying is like sitting in a rocking chair—you rock and rock, but you go nowhere. That is what happens when you worry. You worry and worry but where does that worrying take you? Nowhere. I guess I have had issues with fighting fear in the past, which is something I know God has to release me from. I keep saying that it will take a huge miracle because I have had things happen in my life that created the fear-like environment I live in. However, I know I have to beat the fear because I don't want to bring it into my children's lives or their way of thinking.

When I think back on my life, I think about the fact that I never wanted to be remembered as a fearful person. I have always wanted people to remember me as someone who loved, forgave, and was kind and as one who was courageous and strong, not someone who lived in fear.

CHAPTER 3

THE WHISPER

As I look back on my life, I realize all the things that happened to me were what actually transformed my thinking here in the present. I have always believed that events and circumstances either make us or break us in every big or bad situation. The problem is overcoming the brokenness and allowing the pieces to come together. Life is all about learning from every situation and allowing it to shape us and help us grow.

Now that I think about it, I realize all of the big obstacles in my life were stepping-stones. We all have choices in life. Would we use life's stones to grow and move us forward over the sinking ground or would we choose to fall off the path and lie to waste? I know many times when I fell off my stepping-stone I would lie around and not move forward in growth because I would be so down. I see I have had some major blows that have brought me to my knees. Blows that broke me. There were many times I wondered if I would ever be happy again. The feeling of being in sinking sand is the best way to describe how I would feel. It was like I wanted to move but I couldn't, and the more I struggled, the more I sank. I can't say that I have ever been in quicksand physically, but I have felt like I was there many times spiritually and emotionally. This is the best analogy I can think of to describe my emotions and help give an illustration. When someone falls into quicksand, it's almost impossible to get out without assistance. Every time I found myself being beat by life, the only way I could rise up is if I would first bend the knee. God was always the one to rescue me. Trust me, I have needed some major rescuing.

I'll never forget one particular night that I felt so broken, scared, and fearful knowing I could lose my life. The only reason I lived was because I listened to a small voice that told me to hide. Tom was at home with the kids because I had a meeting with one of my favorite clients. I met my client for a late dinner to go over some advertising plans, and during our dinner, the time got away from me. When I realized it was eleven o'clock, I knew I needed to get home because, as always, I was bringing dinner home for the hubs, and the later it got, the hangrier he would be! I wrapped up the meeting and left to head home.

On my way home, I noticed my gas gauge was low and

the screen said I had seventeen miles to empty. I probably should have filled up the tank prior to my meeting because the last place I wanted to be at midnight was at a gas station. Running my tank to empty was something I did quite often because I dreaded getting gas for some reason but I dreaded even more the idea of being stranded out in the dark with a vehicle that ran out of gas. So, I sighed a huge sigh of relief when my vehicle rolled into the station with only seven miles left. This particular gas station is very close to my home, so I always stopped there for my gas. I felt safe pumping gas and going inside the store because the location is in a good area, plus the station is clean.

As I started filling up my tank, I realized that no customers were inside, so I decided to run in and grab a bottle of antacids to calm my crazy heartburn. When I got inside, I spotted Shelly and Rick together behind the counter. Shelly is my all-time favorite attendant, and because I am a talker, I have gotten to know all the employees at the station.

After I said hello to Shelly and chatted for a minute, I walked over to one of the aisles to look for the medicine. As soon as I turned into the aisle, I heard a whisper say, "Go to the restroom and lock the door—NOW."

How gross! A single gas station bathroom was not a place I ever wanted to enter. I thought the request was weird because it was obviously something I would never do. I started searching the shelf for the antacids when I heard the same request again. This time the tone was a little sterner, like a parent ordering a child to do something, and if the child didn't obey, she would be in trouble. After the second warning, I decided I better listen to the voice/gut feeling I was having. I went straight to the bathroom, shut the bathroom door, and of course, locked it behind me.

Right as I shut the door, I heard a ding—someone had entered the front entrance door. Within a few seconds, yelling started. I quietly stayed in the bathroom like I felt the voice telling me. Not wanting anyone to hear my phone ring and come looking for me, I pulled my phone out of my purse and quickly turned it to silent.

Then the yelling escalated to screams followed by three distinct *pop, pop, pop* sounds. I knew right then what was happening. I froze in place against the bathroom wall and dialed 911. I turned the call volume all the way down and held the phone next to my side. I knew someone was on the other end of the call because it connected, but I was in no position to talk, move, or listen. I just knew I needed to call so they could try to ping my phone or something. I wasn't sure what I was doing other than staying where I was and being as quiet as possible.

After a few minutes of hearing a couple of guys yelling and scrambling around, I heard the front door ding again. I prayed it was the men leaving and not someone else coming in. Suddenly the thought hit me that my SUV was out front with the gas nozzle still in it. *Dear God, please blind their eyes to my vehicle. Please don't let them come back in and look for me.* The prayers I prayed while in freak-out mode must have been heard because the door didn't ding.

I sank to the floor in the corner of the bathroom listening to the silence and the music playing softly over the sound system. After a couple minutes of tense silence, I slowly raised my phone to my ear and whispered, "I think there was a robbery here at the gas station. I heard three gunshots."

The 911 dispatcher asked my exact location and told me to not exit the bathroom until the police arrived and knocked on the door. And that is exactly what I did. Even after I heard another person come in and scream, I didn't move or make a peep. I sat on the floor not even thinking about the fact that there were pieces of wet toilet paper next to me and a strong odor burning my nose. Usually, that is something that would make me cringe, but at this time, I didn't care if I was sitting in it, I wasn't moving. Tears rolled down my cheeks, and my body began to shake with what I'm sure was shock.

Within minutes I heard the sirens, and then a knock on the restroom door. I mustered all the strength I had left and crawled over to the door to open it. I reached up and unlocked the door and slowly cracked it open. The officer looked down at me with such compassion that I couldn't help but crumple back down to the floor.

"You're safe. I've got you. It's okay." He reached down to help me up, and I tentatively place my hand in his. I was scared to walk out of the restroom. I didn't want to see who was shot. I knew someone was dead because after the three shots I only heard two voices yelling orders back and forth to each other.

With the officer's help, I stood and leaned against the doorframe to try and steady myself. I swiped my hand across my face wiping the tears still trickling down my cheeks.

"Are you okay, ma'am?"

"I'm…I'm…worried about…Shelly and Rick." I choked out my words between the sobs that shook my body.

"Who are Shelly and Rick?" The officer placed his hand on my elbow in what I'm sure was a gesture to help keep me standing up. He motioned for me to walk with him towards the store entrance.

I saw blood all over behind the counter where both Shelly and Rick had been standing. I pointed over at the counter and said, "Them."

"I'm sorry. Were they your friends?"

"Yes." My heart sunk. I like to talk to people and love visiting even if it's in the middle of a gas station store. Yes, they were my friends.

I don't doubt that God rescued me that night. I had a lot

of trauma to overcome from the event, and I would like to think that I did overcome major fear that crept into my life, but even to the day of my death, I never stepped back into that gas station. It's kind of like how a person who gets food poisoning will never eat the food that made them sick ever again. This is how I was with that place. I never went back ever again.

As I continue to look back at that night and other events that took place in my life, I can see why so many of my actions were directed out of and by fear. But I didn't want to live my life in fear. Looking back, I guess a part of me could say I regret living in fear. Maybe I should have taken more chances and let go more. My fears are just a few of the things I regretted when I found out that my days on the earth had come to an end.

CHAPTER 4

THE PARTY

Let's jump ahead to the day I ended up in heaven, the day my sweet David turned seven years old. It was his big party day, and we had planned this day for a couple of months. Whenever we had the funds, we liked to really celebrate each kids' birthday in a big way. This year was a year of blessings, so we were able to give all our kids great birthday parties and make plans for an amazing Christmas.

August 10, David's birthday, was a beautiful Saturday. Everything was going as planned. We all woke up early to have breakfast, and then we went to Aunt Julie's to swim, which had been our favorite thing to do all summer! After swimming, we went home to take a break before the big party.

This year David wanted his party at the Jump-N-Play Bounce Barn. Kids loved this place because it was full of every bouncy house known to man and everything revolved around the barn theme. One bounce area had a goat noise that sounded every time someone jumped high enough to hit the button at the top of the moon bounce. Another had a maze that had blown up bulls that would charge and knock you over if you weren't fast enough. We had rented the Bounce Barn from six p.m. to nine p.m. that evening. We would spend the first hour in the Party Barn area where we would eat cake and ice cream and open presents before going to play in the Bounce Barn.

Everyone, young and old, looked forward to parties at the Bounce Barn. As an adult, I honestly have to say I would be all over the place having a blast if it weren't for all of the little kids everywhere. For days before the party, Mark, my nine-year-old, talked about challenging the bouncy bull in the arena. David, the birthday boy, wanted to play knock the chicken over in the bouncy hen house. And Esther, my youngest, was excited to eat the birthday sweets.

Before leaving the house at 5:15 p.m., I told Tom that maybe we should take two cars just in case Elijah became cranky and I needed to take him home. I felt as if my leaving in the second vehicle would save the other little ones from having to leave early as well. Both the hubs and I agreed that having two vehicles would be a good idea, so Tom drove Mark and David in the truck and I followed with Esther and Elijah in the SUV. On the way to the party, we swung by and picked up two of David's best friends because their moms weren't going to be able to make it. Steve and Blake both got in the truck with Tom and the boys. After we picked up the extra riders, we made our way to the party.

We arrived at the party with ten minutes to spare, and only one other friend was there waiting. I started to get nervous because we had eight kids RSVP, and if less showed up, I would have wasted a couple of hundred dollars. But the money wasn't my main concern. My biggest concern was David not having enough friends there to celebrate his birthday. I didn't want him to feel rejected. No mother ever wants her kids to feel rejected. One year we had invited over ten friends to Mark's party and only two kids showed up. That was heartbreaking and something I don't ever want to see any of my kids go through again. Thankfully, by the time David's party began, everyone had made it, minus one whose mom texted and said she was running a little late but ended the text with the promise that Rob would be there.

We started with cake and ice cream. We sang and laughed as Tom jokingly gave David his seven birthday pats on his bottom. Then David started opening gifts. His first gift was from his favorite people outside of our home— G-Pa and Grammy. They always buy him huge Nerf guns so nobody was shocked when he unwrapped the newest and latest multi-shot NERF gun. His next gift was from Blake, one of his best friends, and it was an Xbox game he had wanted. I was shocked because I knew the game cost over sixty dollars new.

Blake had been David's best friend since they first met in kindergarten. They said they knew they were meant to be friends because they both thought the teacher was silly for always calling David by Blake's name and Blake by David's. They couldn't figure out how she confused them because they look nothing alike. Blake's skin is dark and he has dark brown hair while David is pale white with blonde hair. Because that teacher's mishap continued all year, they became the best of friends and to this day they will call each other by the other's name. Blake is an only child and both of his parents make a lot of money in insurance, so while a sixty-dollar game wasn't that big of a deal to them, it was a big deal to us. Remember we have five kids, and even though kids are expensive, I still wouldn't trade them for the world!

One by one, David opened each gift. I could tell he was excited when he was handed the gift from his dad and me, but when he opened the gift, he looked down a little as if he were disappointed. This broke my heart because we had paid a lot for the new game system.

After he was done opening our gift, a Party Barn employee came in and asked, "Are you guys ready to party?" Of course, everyone cheered and took off running to the big open play area.

I carried Elijah on my chest in a swaddle strap, and Esther held my hand as we went to play the arcade games. Esther and I both love Skee-Ball, so of course, we went there first to start playing. After playing the arcade game, Esther decided she was ready to go bounce. Before we left the arcade area, she begged me for some change so she could win a heart necklace. I say "win" with hesitation because it really wasn't a game. It was just a machine that you put a quarter in, twist the dial, and it dispenses a toy. I gave Esther two quarters knowing that the toy dispenser only required one quarter. Esther put her first quarter in and got a pink heart necklace. She was so excited she put a second quarter in, but this time the machine messed up and gave her two heart necklaces—a purple and a red. She looked up at me and asked if I would put the pink necklace on her, which of course I did. After I finished, she said, "Mommy, I have something for you. Hold out your hand and close your eyes." So, I did and I felt her place something in my hand.

"Okay, Mommy, you can open your eyes."

In my hand were both the red and the dark purple necklaces. "Esther, why did you give me your necklaces?"

"Because I have one, silly. Give these to someone extra, extra, extra special, Mommy. But it can't be me because you already gave me mine!"

"Thank you, honey. I will do exactly that." I wrapped my arms around her for a quick hug and then placed the necklaces in my pocket.

Right then, David ran up to us. "Mom, will you accept a challenge to Earthquake Alley?"

"Sure!" I was excited to take on his challenge. "But first, let me ask Dad if he will hold Elijah while we play."

Earthquake Alley is a huge moon bounce that is constantly in motion, and it takes all the leg muscles you can muster up to move around. The object of the game is to touch each one of your animals, either lambs or bobcats, and save them before they deflate. The team that tags the most animals is the winner at the end of the game. Well, of course, David wanted bobcats because they are strong. I love being the lamb because I believe with the lamb you have the upper hand since they are wider and easier to tag.

The bell went off, and so did David. Tag one, tag two on David's side and I hadn't even reached my first lamb. Tag, tag, tag. Three more down on David's side before I finally got my first tag. I tried running to my next lamb, but I wiped out. I tried getting back up, but the moon bounce was working against me, and I only managed to make it up on all fours before toppling over again. I started laughing so hard I almost peed myself, and I could hear others laughing as well. Before I could get up, I heard the buzzer. Game over. Time was up, and David romped on me. I had one tag, and he tagged his entire group of bobcats minus one that deflated before he reached it. Wow, how could I be so terrible at a game? It was great, though, seeing David laugh and rub it in my face about how awful I played. I laughed with him and looked over and noticed the entire birthday party was on the sidelines just giggling away, including Tom. After I climbed across that three-hour leg workout that was really only thirty seconds but sure felt a lot longer, I jumped down.

"Watch out, Mom! Here I come!" David said as he jumped onto my back.

We walked away from that arena together slowly because, let's face it, I was worn out. While I was carrying him, I asked David why he looked so disappointed when he opened his gift. He replied, "Mom, all I really wanted was a gift card so I could purchase gold on my app game. But it's okay. I like my game system."

I thought about how much money I would have saved if I had just bought him what he asked for and not what we wanted for him. I felt awful. I bent down a bit so he could hop off my back. "Honey, before you go play some-where else, I have something small for you. It's small in size but means a lot to me because it was given to me by someone super special. I was instructed that when I got it, I needed to give it to someone extra, extra, extra spe-cial. Now I know this might seem silly, but I want this to be a reminder, a symbol to you, of my love and how I will always listen and be here for you. Any time you are scared or doubting, I want you to hold this tight and remember this moment right now." I handed him the red heart necklace. "David, you are super special and you, along with your brothers and sister, all own my heart. I want you to always remember that."

He smiled as he took the necklace, and I told him I loved him. He gave me a quick hug and then ran off to play.

Right then, Tom walked up with Elijah, who was sleeping, and said, "Honey, looks like you had it handed to you out there." I couldn't help but laugh along with him because I could only imagine how I had looked wobbling around.

Elijah chose that moment to wake up and let out a wail. Tom commented that he had been getting irritable and I knew that he was done with the entire "being out late" (for him) scene. Since he was so young, he still slept most of the time although loud noises startled him awake and the party definitely had its share of loud noises. With an hour left of the party, I told Tom I would take the baby home and he could bring Esther home since she was having way too much fun and making her leave would be like punishing her.

Before leaving, I looked around for Mark, David, and Esther to tell them I was headed home. I spotted them in the middle of catching the animals in the Hurricane Harbor blowout challenge. Elijah's wails were getting louder, so I told Tom to tell them I loved them and I would see them later.

I gave Tom a quick kiss, and off Elijah and I went.

CHAPTER 5

THE DAY MY WORLD STOOD STILL

As I walked to the SUV, Elijah's cries reached a volume that was almost a complete scream, which was not at all like him. I knew he was ready to be home in the quiet, snuggled next to me, but I was sad to leave the party. I loved watching the kids have so much fun in each obstacle course. I also enjoyed seeing them have sweet competitions that led to full-blown laughter. But I knew being a mom meant I had to be ready to answer when duty called, and Elijah was making sure I knew mommy duties were calling.

By the time I reached the car, I had already inspected Elijah's buckles to make sure Tom had him in the car seat correctly and his straps were tight enough. It's not that I didn't trust Tom, but I had noticed a few times that the straps had been a little loose and that, of course, isn't safe. Satisfied that my baby was secure, I snapped his carrier into the car seat base anchored to the seat. After buckling myself in, I turned on my praise and worship music. I always functioned better having a little praise and worship in my system, and I needed it for the drive home. After the music started, Elijah quickly quieted down and fell asleep.

I decided to spend time in prayer and have my quiet time with God on the drive home. First, I prayed for safety over all the kids still at the party, and then I prayed over Tom and asked that God would keep them safe as they drove home. After those prayers, I lifted John up in prayer. John is the only child I worry about because he is out on his own. Since he moved out, I have prayed over him that he will make the right choices in life. I know he has outside influences, so I have learned the only defense in that situation is to pray because once we let them go as parents, there isn't much more we can do but trust God to be with them.

While praying over John, I stopped mid-sentence. Headlights in the distance were aimed directly at me. On my side of the road.

I blinked my eyes to make sure I was seeing correctly. It didn't make sense because concrete barriers divided the turnpike and kept oncoming traffic off the wrong side of the road. I figured I had to be seeing things. I knew the only way a person could be driving on my side of the road was if that person had entered on the "exit only" ramp a little ways down the highway. I regretted the fact that I didn't have my glasses on. I didn't require glasses to drive, but the optometrist had said they would help at night when I drove. A small astigmatism messes with my night driving so maybe I was having issues with my vision.

I was wrong. It wasn't my vision. I was seeing correctly.

A huge truck was barreling the wrong direction down the highway headed straight towards us. I panicked. This was really happening. I moved across two lanes in an attempt to miss the truck, but he switched lanes too. I quickly glanced out the passenger window and realized we were on a bridge so I couldn't swerve off the road to avoid him. I also couldn't stop. I knew my only option was to try and dodge this person who was obviously intoxicated or had a death wish.

Why us? Why did he have to be there at that exact moment when we were headed home? Why didn't God give me a heads up this time and tell me to go a different direction? Thoughts rushed through my head, but they were in slow motion, if that makes sense.

Not knowing what else to do, I yanked the wheel quickly hoping to spin the vehicle and hoping that being hit in the rear of the SUV would be less of a blow than if we were hit head-on. However, the spin wasn't a full turn. We were going too fast, even though I had slowed down immensely, and I knew we could flip. But I wasn't sure at that point what would be safer—let the vehicle flip to try to avoid impact or let it be hit. I knew hitting head-on would be deadly, so I did the only thing I knew to do.

I screamed out to God to help us as the front end of the truck clipped the rear driver's side of the vehicle.

The impact was so powerful. I felt my head hit something, and then I heard nothing but a high pitch whistling sound in my head. It was almost like I went deaf and everything was in slow motion. I looked over and saw my purse in the air with tons of other little things floating with it.

I felt the vehicle go into a spin that was more of a roll. Over and over we went until we broke the barrier of the bridge and went tumbling onto the road below us.

Everything went black for a moment. When I came to, I realized I had been ejected from the vehicle. How I don't know because I'd had my seatbelt on. I am not sure if it was a seat belt malfunction or what. All I knew is somehow I was lying in the middle of the highway with my crushed SUV next to me.

I remember lying there as my world stood still. Time was no more. It felt as if eternity had started and I was stuck in a death position not able to move. My head was tilted towards the SUV and I stared at the pile of metal. I couldn't look anywhere else nor did I want to take my eyes off my SUV because my sweet Elijah was in there. I tried to scream for him but no sound came out. I couldn't move and the pressure in my head was becoming so intense that I thought surely this was the end. It was time to go. I couldn't feel any pain, and I knew that couldn't be good. I couldn't feel my legs, arms, or any part of my body. I couldn't move anything either. All I could feel was the pounding pressure in my head.

Everything within me wanted to run to the SUV and find my baby. I wanted to make sure he was okay, even though I knew it would be a miracle if he were. Part of me hoped his car seat had somehow been ejected like I was because I knew there was no way he had survived inside the crushed up SUV. Deep down I knew his seat, with all its safety features, had not been ejected.

I started praying in my head begging for God to save my baby and begging if he didn't save Elijah then to please take me with him. I couldn't bear to live and my sweet baby not. I begged for all this to be a bad dream and for God to let me wake from it.

As I laid there in my own blood scared to death, a young man calmly walked over to me. He sat down next to my broken body and gently touched my shoulder. He reassured me that someone was on the way to help. I wanted to tell him that I needed to get my baby out of the car but no matter how badly I wanted to speak, nothing came out. The man continued to sit there, calmly reassuring me that everything was going to be okay.

Blood started filling my eyes, and I felt something running out of my ears. I looked at the man with distress. I knew he could see the fear all over my face. He looked up to the heavens and then looked back at me and said a small prayer of peace over me. He asked that God would touch me, and the moment he sent that request to heaven is the moment I felt a release in my head. The pressure eased up, all the pain lifted, and peace fell over me. As soon as the first responders showed up, the man disappeared into the chaos of people that must have been around me the entire time but I never noticed until the young man stood up and walked away. When he left, I started feeling the pressure in my head once again.

The pressure was getting to be too intense and too much to bear, so I closed my eyes. With my eyes closed, I thought about my life and how fast it was being taken from me. I also thought about the stranger. I didn't know who he was or where he came from. All I knew was he had a demeanor about him that brought some sort of peace during what seemed like an eternity.

At that moment in time, as I laid on the concrete road, scared but knowing the end would soon be upon me, my world stood still.

CHAPTER 6

DYING

In the ambulance, I kept slipping in and out of consciousness. I felt my body slowly fading, and each time I came to, I was shocked to find that I was still alive. I wondered if God was going to take me home. I wasn't sure what was happening.

All I knew was I was ready for this horrible nightmare to end. The pain of not knowing where Elijah was and if he was okay was heartbreaking. I started thinking about what I could have done differently, if anything. All the emotions were running through my head, and yet I couldn't move or speak. Then all went dark again.

When I came to the next time, it wasn't like the times before. This time I wasn't me. I mean I was me, but I wasn't there in my body. I was outside of my body hovering over myself in a room with a lot of nurses and a couple of doctors. They were rushing around working on me trying to get my heart to start beating again. I watched as they shocked my body then pumped my chest. They did this multiple times. Finally, after a shock, they had a heartbeat on the monitor, and they raced out of the room with my body. I wasn't sure where they were going because I was already gone. Their efforts were kind but done in vain because I knew I had already left my shell of a body.

I found myself in another room where I saw my family. Watching them grieve was painful, but not like the physical pain I felt earlier while I laid in the middle of the highway. I thought at the time I was losing consciousness because the pressure in my head was too much for my body to handle, but I guess my injuries were much worse and I was actually slowly dying, as I had just witnessed in the other room.

I saw Tom, David, Mark, and Esther in the waiting room. John wasn't there, but he lived farther away and probably hadn't made it yet, if Tom had even been able to reach him. I noticed David squeezing something tight in his hand. I couldn't imagine what he would be holding on to so tightly, but I figured it was something important. I continued to watch as Grandma and Grandpa walked in. Grandma ran over to hug Tom while Grandpa embraced Esther and held her. He whispered something to her, and they left the room hand-in-hand. I figured he was trying to protect her by taking her away from all of the commotion. I couldn't hear the words being said among my family members, but I could feel the words and emotions.

I didn't stay in the waiting room long and within minutes found myself back at our house. When I showed up at the house, I started walking around looking at all the projects and plans I had started but never finished. I thought about all the times I stressed out over silly things when I should have relaxed. The house was completely clean, which usually would make me feel good, but now I didn't feel so good about it. I thought about all the times I cleaned when I could have been playing with the kids or how I had worked hard to keep everything nice when I should have spent more time helping Mark with his homework. I thought about all the times I jumped the kids for getting mud on the clean tile. Oh, the little silly things I regretted. Now, looking back, I wished my house was dirty because that meant my time was not spent on the house but with my family.

I looked over at my desk and saw how unorganized it was. I couldn't help but remember the time Tom, being helpful, cleaned it for me, and I got mad at him for messing up my mess. I always knew where everything was in my mess, but when he cleaned it, I was at a loss and became completely upset. Instead of getting mad, I should have thanked him. He was trying to show me love, and I showed him anger in response to his sweet action.

I walked around the house for what seemed like hours but may have been only minutes. Memories, both good and bad, raced through my mind. I realized there were so many things I would have changed if only I had known my life was going to be cut short. I would not have worried about sleep. I would have spent more time doing hair or nails with Esther. I would have made sure I spent time helping David learn new songs on the piano or watching Mark as he played his video games. I regretted the small things, the things I could have easily changed and made time for but didn't.

Next, I found myself at my brother's house. He was working, as usual, while his wife was trying to get his attention. I could tell by her expression that he still had no clue I had been in an accident. He was so out of touch with my life that I think once he finds out I am gone he will finally feel the loss I felt a long time ago with him. Not that I want him sad. I just hate that it will take my death for someone to realize how much they should have appreciated me while I was here. For that matter, it obviously took my own death for me to realize how many things I took for granted. Life is silly like that. We see things so differently while living because we get so caught up in the mundane and the expectations of life that we forget to keep our focus on the big picture—LIFE and LIVING that life to the fullest.

My mind drifted back to all the times I should have taken trips with the family, but instead, I worried about what bill to pay next. I should have lived and made awesome memories together with our children instead of working constantly. I know I had to work so that we could live, but did we need that big house we had? We probably could have made do with something smaller. Maybe a house on some land so we could take the ATVs out and go off-roading together. But now it was too late. I should have lived more and worried less about what others would think if my house wasn't clean or what people thought of me as a mother. All my ridiculous worries confronted me at once.

I had wasted so much time in fear, and now my life was over. I wanted to cry out to God and ask for forgiveness, but then I wondered if I was stuck in hell on earth, a hell that was putting me in a life of living in past mistakes. As soon as that thought came to mind, I found myself in the church our family had visited a few times.

The church service had started, so I decided it must have been morning. As I stood in the back not being noticed at all, I looked up at the prayer screen and saw my name. The congregation was lifting me up in prayer, which, of course, didn't make sense because why pray for someone who has died? Or maybe they were praying for my family? I didn't know, but it seemed like a nice gesture considering I only attended there for about a month before my death. Anyways, I didn't understand why I was there or how they knew to pray for me, but I did notice more now in this church than I had seen before. A bright aura surrounded the stage. It was peaceful, and I felt it pulling me towards it. The more I looked at it, the more I became part of it. At that moment, I realized where I was....

CHAPTER 7

HEAVEN BOUND

That's when I found myself in heaven. I knew it was heaven because a peace fell over me and a weight was lifted. Everything was white all around and then a new spectrum came into focus. I turned and saw fields of flowers full of flowers and colors I had never seen before. I was in complete awe and very at peace. I knew I had finally made it to the place I had worked so hard to enter. At that moment, I realized I had lived a righteous life. The only thing that kept spinning in my head was "here I am."

As I was taking in all the beauty and an aroma that smelled almost like lavender, I saw beautiful trees that were full of vibrant colored blooms. They were waving around as if the wind were blowing but I couldn't feel the wind. I could tell they were talking and alive. I saw life in everything. Things I never thought of as being "alive" before.

The ground was soft beneath my bare feet. It almost

felt like I was walking on a soft comforter filled with down feathers. It felt amazing, like being in a dream you would never want to wake from, but I knew this wasn't a dream. This was real. I felt excited. All the fear I used to feel thinking I would mess up and not make it to heaven faded and went away. By the grace of God, I had made it.

Just as I was about to fall back to lay in the beautifully colored flowers I noticed a man full of light walking towards me in the distance. All the words I knew on earth could not explain His glory. Oh, the glory I felt being in his presence!

He was walking towards me, and I could hear him speaking to me, but not with his voice, not the way we speak here on earth. It was like I could feel and hear His thoughts. He said, "My child, you are here but only for a moment. This is my gift I am giving you. A gift because I love you."

As He came closer, I noticed he was carrying something or someone. Elijah. He had our son Elijah in His hands. At that moment I had the confirmation that not only had I died but Elijah did as well. My son was only a month old when we were in our wreck, but in the arms of the Son of God, he looked to be a little older, wiser, and more alert.

As I ran to Jesus, my eyes stayed fixed on the sight of Him holding my son. The moment I reached them, I fell to the ground grabbing the hem of His garment. I knew I had heard Him say I was only here for a moment, but I didn't want that moment to end. I begged Him to not make me leave, to let me stay. I didn't want to leave His presence nor the splendor and beauty of heaven. And my baby boy. How could I leave him?

I had watched videos where people died and God gave them a choice. The people always chose to return to earth. That was a choice I knew I never would make, because if I made it to heaven once, I didn't want to chance not making it again. I wanted a chance to choose, but I could tell I wasn't going to get a chance to choose like the others.

As I begged within, He heard me and said, "This is my gift because I love you and because I love your son David. Because of him, I am sending you back. David has made a life-changing decision, a promise to me that he will hold if I return you. My sending you back is saving your son's life."

I begged Jesus to keep me. I wanted so badly to save my son's life. I pleaded with the Father, saying "I cannot leave here without my baby." I then reminded God of the prayer I always prayed asking that I leave the earth before any of my children. When I finished reminding Him, He once again explained that this was a gift. He was answering my prayer, yet He was also answering the prayers of others.

I looked at Elijah resting in the arms of Jesus, and I knew I was going to have to leave my baby in heaven. As those thoughts went through my mind, Jesus said, "My daughter, he is in good hands. I love him more than you could ever love him, and because of that, he had to leave earth early. Because of my love for you and for him, I had to take him now. Remember, my child, I will only give you what you can handle, and this, my daughter, you will handle because of my gift. If I were to let him stay on earth, the future that was going to take place wasn't something you could handle. I am bringing him home early, but I am also allowing you to see how much I love both him and you. This will also help you understand that he will always be in good hands. Look around you, my child."

I pulled my gaze away from my baby's beautiful face to look around, and I noticed people everywhere in the field. I wasn't sure where they had come from because they hadn't been there moments before. As I was trying to take everything in, a woman walking with a young man a short distance away caught my attention. She turned her head towards me and smiled a smile I would know anywhere. If I could have cried tears of joy in heaven, I would have at the sight of my mother. She looked young, healthy, happy, and free of cancer. The handsome young man walking with her appeared to be in his early twenties. I wasn't sure exactly who the blond-haired, blue-eyed man was, but I knew he resembled the guy who had sat next to me on the highway while waiting for the first responders to show up.

"Go on, my child. Go see your mom."

I took off running and threw my arms around my

mother. I couldn't believe my mom was finally holding me again. I had waited for so long to feel her arms around me and had missed that feeling ever since the day she died. After my Mom had passed, I had felt like an orphan on earth and now I had her once again.

After a long embrace, my mom stepped back and said, "I want to introduce you to your son."

I looked at the young man and instantly recognized the familiar features that all my kids had. I also realized at that moment that he was the man who had sat with me on the road and gently spoke to me and helped me deal with the pain I felt after the wreck.

"Hi Mom, I have dreamed of this day many times, the day you would finally meet me and see that I was a boy, your boy, the boy you lost when I was only three months old in your womb."

Feelings I couldn't explain overwhelmed me. Memories of my miscarriage had stuck with me over the years. I knew I had lost a child, but I never knew if the baby was a boy or a girl, and because of that, my heart always felt as if a piece of me were missing. I looked at this handsome man, and he grabbed me with the strongest heartfelt hug a human could ever feel. We held each other for what seemed like an eternity and I would have loved for it to have been.

As we pulled back to look at each other again, I looked him in the eye and asked, "My boy, what is your name?"

"You never gave me a name, but up here they call me Micah because the Father said I have a beautiful, humble heart." I know they say there are no tears in heaven, but my heart sank when I realized I didn't give my beautiful son a name. I know Micah felt my thought because he continued, "Mom, please don't feel guilty. You had no clue, and I never held that against you. Plus, I knew you would love the name the Father gave me because you always prayed and asked the Father for names when you had my brothers and sister. This time the Father just named me directly."

I stood there in awe of this gift God was giving me.

My mom told me how proud she was of me, my family, and my children and how very impressed she was with my husband. She was glad I had listened to God because this man was ordained and brought here for me specifically. Mom told me of the times she had visited my children in their dreams and how she caressed them while they slept. She also said she was there the day I was in trouble in the gas station. It was she who had whispered in my ear telling me to go to the restroom. Two lives were lost that day, and it easily could have been three, except for the feeling I had deep down to go hide in the restroom. Now I know it was the gentle whispers of my mother taking care of me that saved my life that day. God allowing her that visit to intervene was another gift from Him.

Micah told me about the times he would sit next to

me and just watch me work. He said he would see me cry and he would save the tears so that part of me could be with him. He pulled out a beautiful crystal box filled with diamonds. "Mom, this is every tear you have cried since the day I turned five here in heaven. God granted me this request. He usually saves the tears, but because he saw my heart and my desire to know you, He gave this to me. Every time you have cried for the last seventeen years, I was there to catch your tears. I spoke to you many times, but I don't think you heard me. I know you love me because God showed me your heart. I felt what you went through the day you lost me. You cried for months, and you didn't understand, but hopefully, you will see now that God had a plan for me here in heaven just like He does for my baby brother Elijah. I hope you can understand that when you go back. I know you will cry more tears when you return, but I want you to remember that every time you do, I will be there. And one day Elijah will join me. I know he owns a part of your heart, and because of that, this I will share."

When Micah was done explaining his heart to me, I realized how great of a man he had become and that he had been in the best hands all along. Jesus returned to my side with Elijah in His arms. I knew the time was coming for me to return to earth, but not one part of me wanted to leave. I could feel the begging taking place in my heart, but I could see in the eyes of Jesus that I had to leave.

Before leaving I asked Jesus to please keep me on the right path so that I may return one day. I couldn't bear to live my life away from Him and the ones I love. Then I looked at Jesus and asked if I could hold Elijah one last time.

As Jesus handed my baby boy over to me, He said, "Because of my love for you and my love for little Elijah, I want you to know that I had my angels come in and pick up Elijah before the impact of the wreck. His angels brought him directly to me, and he has been with me since. He never felt any pain. I protected him from the pain. I do this for many of my children because of my love for them and their parents. I am telling you this so you can go through the rest of your life knowing that my angels were there with you and I was waiting here for you. I want you to always know I am with you. My angels surround you, and when you call on me, I hear you. I heard you when you cried out. I sent Micah, your son, to sit with you during your last minutes on earth because my love for you is bigger than you can ever imagine. I felt your pain the day I died on the cross, a pain that was hard to bear, but my love surrounds that pain and swallows it up in victory. When you go back to earth, I want you to remember this and live your life in that victory I am giving you. I am releasing you from the fear that has bound you for so long because my love is big. This is part of my gift, a gift you are given because of a promise."

I held Elijah tightly like my life was being taken fully

away from me. My desire to stay was so strong that I wasn't sure how I would ever let go. I felt my strength starting to leave, and the Father touched my elbow, lifted me, and said, "My strength is what will hold you up. My love will be with you and my heart is yours. Trust me and know that I am with you always."

I kissed Elijah and handed him to the Father. I turned and gave Mom and Micah one last hug and kiss. And then I closed my eyes and released Jesus's garment I was holding tight in my right hand. I felt Him touch me, and I whispered "I love you" as I left.

CHAPTER 8

THE RETURN

I laid in a bed that was nowhere near as soft and comfortable as the heavens. I heard the Father whisper to me, "Remind David of the promise he made." I had no desire to open my eyes. I did not want to move knowing that my body was severely injured from the wreck and knowing pain would set in as soon as the meds were out of my system.

I sensed people were in the room, but I really didn't care. I was still trying to grasp what had just happened. I had left heaven, and I wasn't completely excited about being back on earth. Every bone in my body wanted to go back to heaven. Not that I didn't want to be with my family here on earth. I adore every single one of them, but I knew they would be fine without me. I wasn't sure how I was going to function knowing I had left something so glorious. God said that was my gift, but I didn't want my gift to end. I wanted to hold onto it forever, or at least for a little while longer. However, I had no choice. I had to return because God has greater plans than I do.

So, here on earth is where I found myself, laying in a hard hospital bed with my legs wrapped up and what felt like heavy blankets on me. I could hear Tom in the room and David's soft whisper as he quietly spoke. I felt the presence of someone else in the room too, but who that person was I didn't know. I heard a machine next to me making soft pumping noises and figured it was attached to my breathing tube. The tube in my throat was uncomfortable to the point that I wanted to yank it out, but my body was too weak to move.

I laid there with my eyes shut just listening to the noises in the room. Tom was talking about the last time he saw me and how happy I was at the party. Then his tone shifted, and he said how sorry he was for not hugging me and telling me that he loved me when I left that night. He kept blaming himself over and over for the accident because if he would have taken the time to hug me, I would have left a few minutes later and maybe avoided the truck. I wanted to tell him it was okay and that I knew he loved me, but my body was too weak to move or to speak. So, I just laid there and listened.

I heard David quietly crying blaming himself because it was his party I had left. Then a voice that sounded familiar, but I couldn't figure out, kept speaking over David telling him that none of this was his fault. I could tell David wasn't listening to the voice because I could feel his sorrow. Every ounce of my being wanted to wrap him in my arms and reassure him that it was okay. None of this was his fault, but again I felt no strength to move. I drifted to sleep listening to the whispers and noises in the room.

I don't know how long I slept, but it seemed like a long time, maybe a day or two. When I awoke, I had a different feeling. The tube was no longer in my throat, yet my throat felt horrible. It felt like the insides were almost touching each other like the time my throat had swelled from strep. I still didn't have the strength to open my eyes, so I listened to the sounds in the room again. I could hear Tom, my sweet David, and my outgoing son Mark. I also heard that familiar voice again and someone else talking.

"Mom, Mom!" I heard the urgency in Mark's voice. "I know you can hear me. Will you squeeze my hand and let me know?"

I didn't realize I was holding his hand, but the moment he said that, I tried with all of my might to squeeze his hand.

"Dad, did you see that?" David's typically quiet voice rose with excitement. "Her pointer finger moved!"

"Yes, I did."

I couldn't understand why they were so excited about a little movement, so I tried to open my eyes to see them and to see how bad of shape I was really in. That's when I realized I couldn't open my eyes. Fear started to take over. Everything was dark. Was I blind? I tried to talk, but my throat hurt, and I felt another tube or something rubbing inside it.

"Relax, Sherrie." A woman's voice that I didn't recognize spoke. "You are in the hospital. You are hurt, but you are going to be okay. Your eyes are swollen shut. We checked your vision, and everything looks like it will be fine once the swelling is gone. Do you remember what happened to you? Can you move your index finger if you do?"

Why would she think I couldn't remember? Of course, I remembered. If I could tell her all the things I had seen since the accident, she would be amazed. But all I could do at the moment was move my finger. That movement and the excitement were all I could take. I was tired and worn out. It was strange because even though I had just woken up, I felt like I could instantly fall asleep again. Then the nurse informed me that I had medicine in my body that would make me feel sleepy and that it was okay to sleep. So, I did. I slept.

When I woke, I felt like I had cold compresses on my eyes. With all of the pain medication in my system, I really couldn't tell if they were actual compresses, cold hands, or just me imagining something was there. The moment I woke, I tried to move. This time my head moved a little. It was tight, but I was able to move it.

The same woman's voice I had heard the night before said, "It's okay. Relax. We are trying to get the swelling down so you can open your eyes. We know this will make you feel better. We want you to see your sweet family that has been here day and night waiting for you to get better."

I guess I smiled a little because my reaction made her happy. I could hear the smile in her voice as she spoke to whoever else was in the room.

I felt a small hand on my arm, and then David whispered how much he loved me and how sorry he was. An ache built up inside me. I wanted so badly to hug him and tell him to quit blaming himself. None of this was his fault, but I guess being seven, and the timing of the accident, made my sweet boy take the blame of the world on his shoulders. Something I would gladly remove if I could just speak and hug him. I tried saying David's name and telling him I loved him, but it sounded like soft grunts and weird moaning noises instead of words.

I heard a shuffling noise on my other side, and I figured it was Mark. I tried to turn my head towards him. "It's okay, Mommy. We know you love us, and we know you are going to get better and come home to us soon. We can't make it without you."

"Yeah, Honey, I don't think the boys can handle my cooking much longer." They all giggled at Tom's silly joke.

Really? That is all you miss? I couldn't help but think

that thought. But I know my husband and how he always likes to lighten the mood. He makes silly statements to try and make everyone feel better in the room. He even does this when he is nervous and has nothing else to say. After twenty-three years, I know my hubs all too well, so I couldn't fault him for the joke.

Then that familiar voice spoke that I had heard multiple times when I had been awake. "Sherrie, we are all praying for you at church. I want you to know that you are going to get better quicker than any doctor could ever predict and you will be home soon."

The moment the words came out of his mouth I thought, "Wow, Lord, I must be really bad if the doctors aren't predicting a good outcome." This is just like me to analyze the words over the message of what is being spoken. This voice was trying to speak peace and blessings over me, but I took the words and looked deeper into the meaning. I can't say that is a good habit, but it is something my mom raised me to always do. My mom was a negotiator for the government, and she instilled these words into my head when I was old enough to understand—"Listen when people speak because their words are telling you more if you truly listen. Everyone always gives himself or herself away when you listen."

After fully analyzing the words spoken, I decided I better say a silent prayer. " Dear Lord, a beautiful gift you gave me, one I didn't deserve. But I ask this of you, if you would please let me see and speak, let healing take place as a new gift for sending me back. Let my healing be greater and quicker than anyone could ever think. Let your miracle shine and let those around see your works and let glory be given to you."

After that short prayer, I laid there for a while listening to all the chatter in the room and then slowly fell back to sleep.

CHAPTER 9

THE NEW MIRACLE

When I awoke, I felt the relief. A bunch of pressure had been removed from my eyes, head, and nose. I tried opening my eyes, and for the first time since being back to earth, I saw light and colors. My eyes did not open very far and things were a little blurry, but I couldn't help but be excited that I could see.

I tried to speak, and my first words since the wreck were "Hey, guys, I'm back." (I felt I needed to lighten the air and give a little comedy since laughter was hard to find at this time.) My voice was weak and raspy, like an almost inaudible whisper, but at least actual words came out this time. The room started buzzing with excitement as everybody started talking at once. David, Mark, and even Esther were in the room along with Tom, Grandma, and Grandpa.

I smiled a bit or at least attempted to because my lips felt kind of weird. "I love you all very much."

A hush fell over the room, and Mark said, "We love you too, Mom."

"Honey," Tom's voice cracked slightly. "I have something I need to tell—"

"I know….I saw Elijah with Jesus." Tears flowed down my cheeks. "He is okay. I saw Jesus holding him and I was able to give him one last hug and kiss. He is okay."

My heart fully broke in that moment. I knew our son was okay, but the pain of not having him with us was so immense that I felt if I died right then and there, it would be okay. I remembered the words from the Father when He said I would be able to handle it now, but later I wouldn't have been able to handle it. Thinking about those words, I reminded myself that God promised I could handle the pain and sorrow. I didn't feel like I was capable, but I held tightly to the promise that said I was going to be okay. I was also holding onto the gift that had shown me my baby was okay, even better than okay. He was going to be raised by the best I could wish or ask for— the heavenly realm.

I took a deep breath, fought back the tears, and said, "God is good…God is good, and I thank Him for my gift."

Of course, nobody in the room understood what I was saying. They probably assumed it was the medicine talking, but I was fully aware of what I was saying and I meant every word. God is good. All the excitement that had been in the room just minutes prior turned into cries and heartbreak.

A nurse who was in the room asked, "You saw Jesus?"

Everyone got quiet. It was a question of awe and wonder.

"Yes, and so much more." My voice was soft and faint. All my strength was gone. "After I rest, I will tell you more."

The tears I couldn't hold back anymore ran down my face as I closed my eyes to sleep once more.

After a while, and again I don't know how much time passed, I heard Mark say, "Dad, can you not just wake Mom?"

"She will wake when her body lets her. Be patient. She needs her rest."

I slowly opened my eyes to find an audience quietly waiting. Mark, David, Tom, Grandma, Grammy, and a nurse were all in the room. Grandma gave me a sheepish grin and told me she had refused to leave with Esther and Grandpa because she wanted to hear what all I had to say. Grammy nodded in agreement and said she had to be there too because she knew whatever I saw was going to be amazing and a miracle.

Then the nurse said, "Wait one second. I need to get Doctor Gray." Within a minute, the nurse and a doctor came rushing back into the room.

Dr. Gray walked over and stood next to my bed. "Sherrie, it's so great to see you awake. How are you feeling?"

"I have been better."

"It's a miracle you made it out of that crash, but from what I've seen, you are a fighter and you have many fighting alongside you."

The words he said didn't make me feel any better because the thought that ran through my head immediately after he spoke was "Does he not think Elijah was a fighter since he didn't make it?" I knew the doctor wasn't meaning anything rude by his comment and that God was fully in control of all who made it in that crash, but I struggled to grasp the fact that I was here and my son was not.

The doctor continued, "So, I hear you saw Jesus holding Elijah?"

"Yes, and I saw a lot more."

"Would you mind telling us? We would all love to hear. And I know Nurse Kelly has stayed way past the end of her shift so she wouldn't miss what you had to say." He must have noticed my eyes closing because he added, "But if you are tired and can't tell us now, we can all wait."

The moment those words left his mouth I could hear everyone in the room take a deep breath like "how dare you?" Their anticipation was high, and I could feel it all around me.

"Honey, what did you see?"

I could tell that Tom wasn't going to let me sleep. They had waited long enough. I opened my eyes and looked around at everyone. When I focused on Dr. Gray, I realized he looked very familiar and I had seen him before, but I couldn't figure out where.

"Do you want me to tell you everything from the beginning?" I noticed my voice sounded stronger. I didn't feel as weak as I had earlier, but I knew my energy wouldn't last long.

They all chimed in with a big "YES" as if they had rehearsed it a few times. Yes, they wanted to hear it all.

"The night I was rushed to the hospital, I left my body the moment my heart stopped the very first time. I hovered high in the room over myself in a peaceful transient state. I saw you, Doctor Gray." I slowly turned my head to look at him. "You were giving orders and telling the others 'Again…Again.' You kept saying you weren't going to let me go. After my heart showed a heartbeat on the machine, you had them rush me out of the room to somewhere else, but my spirit was already gone. I watched my body leave the room, but my spirit didn't follow."

"I remember that night," Dr. Gray said. "It took a few tries to start your heart again. You gave us quite the scare. When your heart started beating and appeared to be stable, we sent you to surgery. But I'll let you continue."

I turned my head slightly to look at Tom. "I saw you in the waiting room pacing, and I'm not sure, but I think you were praying. I've never seen you pray, but you were pacing and muttering with your head down."

Tom nodded his head, and I knew my observation was right. I continued, "David was bent over on his knees praying hard and clasping something. I couldn't see what was in his hand, but he was holding it tight. Mark was facing the corner of the room. All I could see was his back, but I could hear his loud cries. Grandpa walked in, hugged Esther, who was crying, and then took her somewhere else."

"Grandpa took her to the cafeteria for ice cream," Grandma said quietly. "He thought she could use the distraction, and Tom didn't have the capacity at the time to console her too." She placed her hand on top of the blanket covering my legs and patted my leg. "He was a mess thinking he had lost you."

"Then I was gone. I found myself back at the house. It was eye-opening for me. I saw all the mistakes I had made in my life and felt guilty for wasted time. Time I could have been spending with all of you. After that, I was at my brother's house. I don't fully understand yet why I went there. He was working as usual and not really here or there, just somewhere lost in his train of thoughts. I felt bad for him for I saw more and knew he was meant for greatness. He just held himself back for some reason.

"A few seconds later, I found myself surrounded by a light with clouds all around. As I turned, I started to see more—fields of colors, plants, and flowers I had never seen in my life. The colors were amazing and brilliant. They were colors I can't explain because I don't think they exist here on earth. Everything was peaceful, alive, and beautiful.

"In the distance, I saw Jesus carrying Elijah, and in that moment, I realized Elijah didn't survive the accident. I talked with Jesus quite a bit. He was calm, kind, and you could feel his love. It was powerful.

"After that, I saw my mom. She was with Micah."

"Wait, Mom," Mark interrupted. "Who is Micah?"

"He is your oldest brother."

Mark raised an eyebrow. "What? I didn't know I had a brother in heaven named Micah."

I turned to look at Tom and could see the recognition on his face. He knew Micah was our baby we had lost many years ago. I saw the pain in his eyes, and I knew he was remembering trying to help me after our loss and telling me constantly it wasn't my fault even though I blamed myself.

"That was our first pregnancy, and we were so excited to be new parents, but then at three months, I lost the baby. I had no clue if I was having a boy or a girl, but now I know. He is a handsome young man, and he was raised in heaven. God named him Micah because we never named him." Tom started crying, and I knew he felt the same guilt I did for never naming our son. "Tom, sweetheart, don't worry. Micah doesn't hold it against us. He loves us very much and he showed me this love when I visited him in heaven."

I told everyone how Micah visits all the time and how my mom was there the day of the robbery. I told the kids that Nana, my mom, was very proud of them and loved them with all her heart even though they had never met her. I promised to tell them more stories about Nana when I felt better.

Grandma, my stepmom, started crying uncontrollably at this point. In the back of the room, both Nurse Kelly and another nurse who had entered the room shortly after I started my story were crying quietly.

Not wanting to leave anything out and feeling my energy draining, I told them about how Jesus let me hold Elijah one last time and how I kissed him and then Jesus sent me back. I explained that I was sent back because of a prayer, a promise. I moved my head slightly to look at David and he lost it. He cried harder than I had ever seen him cry. Mark went over to David and hugged him tightly. They just held each other, taking it all in.

Tom sat on the edge of my bed in complete shock. After a few moments, he finally spoke and asked, "Did Elijah look okay? Was he hurt?"

I told him Elijah looked better than okay. I wished so badly that I could explain how amazing Elijah looked, but no words could adequately describe anything I saw or witnessed in the heavenly realm.

"I haven't started planning his funeral," Tom said as his

hand covered mine. "I couldn't think of doing any of it without you. I don't even know where to start."

Grandma regained her composure and said, "I called some places and the funeral services were donated and the casket too. The cemetery gave us a spot for Elijah but asked that we cover the cost of the opening and closing of the grave." She went on to explain that the nurses had suggested she call and ask because they had heard of places donating to families who lost babies unexpectedly.

After telling my story, I was physically and emotionally spent. I fought to keep my eyes open, but all I wanted was to sleep. Doctor Gray who had tears in his eyes finally spoke and said, "Before you go back to sleep, you need to try eating some soft foods. We want to get you off of the feeding tube."

I agreed and ate a little bit of applesauce that Tom fed to me on a spoon. It was all I could handle. As I closed my eyes, I heard Doctor Gray walk back into the room.

"I've been a doctor for a long time, and I've never seen or heard such a miracle in my life. I knew there was a God before, but now I have no question or doubt because of everything Sherrie described in her story. There's just no way she could have known that she died on that table other than what she told us. And she knew the details. She knew what I said that night. She's alive only by a miracle. I know God had a plan for all this."

After listening to Dr. Gray, I fell asleep, and this time my rest was full of dreams and peace, a peace I hadn't felt since the day I left heaven.

THE PROMISE

Later the next morning when I woke up, the pain was noticeable, but I also felt the healing taking place in my body. I asked Nurse Kelly if there was any way I could try to sit up because I needed to move a little. She told me moving would hurt pretty bad, but once I positioned myself into a new spot, the pain would subside. She suggested waiting about twenty minutes before trying since I had just received a dose of morphine. I took her advice and didn't rush the request.

While waiting to sit up, I talked with Tom. He told me that his work had him on FMLA so he was going to be there by my side as long as I needed him. The moment he said that, the memory of the times I hadn't been so nice to him struck me. "Tom, I need to ask you to forgive me for all the times I was mean to you or didn't give you the attention you desired. Those times when I was stressed out and couldn't focus on you. Please forgive me. I also want to thank you for the time you cleaned my desk and I got mad at you."

"There's no need to apologize. We are in this life together. I love you, and I forgive you."

"My time in heaven made me realize how superficial many things I used to do were. I want to change. I need to change. I felt a little hell on earth before I visited heaven, and I don't ever want to feel like that again. I want to live life fully. If I can ever get out of this hospital, I want to go on trips. I want to spend time with our children. Real time. I want us to do things we will look back on and smile."

"Honey, we are going to have to bury our little Elijah first." He broke down, and I felt his pain as he cried.

That's when I told him that Elijah didn't feel any pain and that God took him before the impact. That made Tom cry even more, and he asked how could I know such a thing. I explained to him all that Jesus told me and showed me. "It's going to be hard to move forward without Elijah, but every time I start to get sad, I remember his face and Jesus holding him tight. I know that's hard to comprehend and not something you want to hear, but he is being taken very good care of. He has so many up there who already love him. It hurts that we can't be the ones to raise him, but he will be there when we leave this earth, and we will see him again. We just can't mess it up here because I know where I want to go when I leave this earth again. No place can ever compare to the heavenly realm."

After I spoke those words, Nurse Kelly asked if I was ready to sit up. I had forgotten she was in the room. She had tears running down her face as she slowly helped me move to a new position. She arranged the pillows behind me and then quietly left the room.

When my pain subsided some, I asked Tom where the kids were.

"Esther is at your parents. She hasn't been able to go back to school yet. Mark is taking a nap at G-Pa's house, and David will be here shortly. He went to take a nap at G-Pa's house too but asked that I let him know when you woke up so that Grammy could bring him back. So, he is on his way here now."

I was really wanting to know about John, but I didn't want to ask outright and feel the heartache in case he didn't want to see me. Tom must have read my thoughts because he said, "John came up twice to see you. Both times you were sleeping, and he didn't want to wake you. He asked me to tell you that he loves you and that he will be back again to try to catch you when you are awake."

After hearing that, my heart was happy. I missed my John and was hoping that he would at least visit, but I wanted him to come because of his desire to visit not because I requested him to.

"I need to close my eyes for a second. If I fall asleep, promise me that you will wake me as soon as David gets here." Tom nodded his agreement, and I closed my eyes. I did not understand why I was so tired all the time, but it seemed like every time I got some sleep, I woke up feeling a little better than the time before. So sleep was good in my books.

I must not have fallen into a deep sleep because I heard David's voice in the hallway and opened my eyes. When he entered the room, his eyes lit up when he saw me sitting up looking at him. I could feel his depth of love for me. He hugged Tom and then sat tentatively on the edge of the bed. I reached out and patted a spot closer to me that he could scoot to. "Hi, baby, I'm so glad I get to see you again. Maybe Dad can give us some time alone just you and me. Would you like that?"

David nodded his head and looked at Tom.

"Sure thing. This is actually a great time for Grammy and me to run out and grab some food. Can you take care of Mommy while I'm gone?"

"Of course, Dad!"

I waited for Tom to leave the room, and then I placed my hand on top of David's. "Honey, Jesus asked me to remind you of the promise you made Him."

As soon as those words left my lips, David broke down in tears. He regained his composure after a moment, so I asked why he was sad.

"Because, Mom, that means God heard my prayers. He really heard me."

"Yes, honey, He did, and He told me it was because of your promise that He was sending me back."

David started crying uncontrollably like I had never seen him cry before. This time he couldn't even gain enough composure to talk. I gave him some time to cry, and when he was getting his breath, I asked, "Is it okay if I ask what your promise was?"

"Jesus…Jesus didn't tell you?" He looked at me in surprise when I shook my head no. He ducked his head a bit and said, "I want to tell you, but I'm scared you will get mad at me, Mommy."

I assured my son that I would not get upset and that he could talk to me.

He started telling me about the day he met Damien and Lucas, two brothers who attend his school. They are outgoing smart boys who were fun to hang out with and they always made David feel welcomed when they played at recess. One day, they got into a debate about God and if he was real. David, of course, spoke his beliefs that I had taught him. The two brothers were raised by a strong atheist and had their own reasons as to why God wasn't real. I guess they gave such a great argument about why God wasn't real that David started to question God. The more he hung out with the two brothers, the more he started to think as they did. He admitted that when I taught the Bible at home or talked about God, he would roll his eyes deep down. He was to the point of all belief being lost, and he was okay with that. But he never wanted to tell me because he knew how much I believed in God and how I wanted my children to believe as well.

The entire time David was telling me his story, my heart was breaking. I had no clue that my son had given up all hope, trust, and faith in God. I started to cry as the feeling that I had messed up overwhelmed me.

"Mommy, don't be upset, there was nothing you could have done. It's because of my friends, not you." He paused and then said, "But, Mommy, that all changed the night of my party. I knew you died. I knew you were gone, and I begged God to let you come back. I promised him that if He would give you back, I would live my life for Him every day I lived. And I meant every word. God gave you back, and that's the day I gave my heart fully to God like you taught us. I know God heard me. He gave me the gift of you, and my gift to Him is me. I will keep my promise, Mommy, because His love is BIG."

I melted at his words and became a crying mess. His words were the words I had heard Jesus speak, and I knew when David spoke them he meant them with all he had. Now, I fully understood what the Father meant by my coming back to save his life. It wasn't literal; it was spiritual. It was a life given to God. A gift because of the promise. It was a true gift of life.

It took me a bit before I could speak again, but I finally asked, "Honey, that night you were in the room and I was back with the doctors, what were you holding in your hand?"

David smiled. He pulled the red heart necklace out of his pocket and said, "The thing that meant everything to me. My special heart."

THE RELEASE

Since I had improved so much, the doctors were finally allowing people other than family members to visit. I was looking forward to it because I really needed a pick me up since being in the hospital for what seemed like forever was starting to wear on me.

After my time with David, my first set of visitors was a sweet, elderly couple I had befriended over the last year named Joe and Rose Heart. They were great friends, always ready to help when our family was struggling. One time, a few months before Elijah was born, Tom got sick and I didn't feel well. They came over, spent time with the kids so Tom and I could rest, and they helped clean the house.

When Joe walked into the hospital room, I could tell he was trying to be chipper and keep the mood lively. He smiled like always, but I sensed his sadness. Rose could never hide her feelings, and the moment she walked in the room, she broke down in tears. Multiple times, she said how sorry she was. I assured her I was okay and we were going to be okay. I knew she was referring to the loss of Elijah, but I couldn't speak about that yet because I was still going through my own battle. Even seeing and knowing my sweet baby was with Jesus, it still hurt not having him or holding him in my arms. Every time I felt the hurt, I said, "God, I know he is with you, and I trust you. I love you BIG and will continue to love you. Thank you for taking care of my son."

Joe and Rose visited for a while but left when Ellie and Sky showed up. Ellie and Sky are a cute newlywed couple that Tom and I had met a few years ago. They are fun to hang out with because they are just blunt and carefree. They brought a ton of yummy looking food to the room, but my stomach was still adjusting to food so I didn't eat anything. However, David, Tom, and Mark who was now in the room sure took advantage of the feast.

The entire day was filled with visits, gifts, and blessings from others. I felt bad when I dozed off during a few visits, but I knew I needed the rest to heal. By the end of the day, though, I was worn out and ready to sleep. Of course, anyone who has ever stayed in a hospital knows that good sleep doesn't come at night or anytime. But no matter what, I planned to make the best out of what I had. The boys went back to G-Pa and Grammy's house for the night, where they had been staying since my wreck. Esther stayed with Grandma and Grandpa. She came to visit quite often, but she never stayed long. She is like her grandpa and needs to be moving and can't stay in one place for too long. Knowing all my kids were in good hands helped me rest, and I fell asleep with Tom by my side. The next morning I woke up to find Tom waiting patiently for me to wake and start the day.

"Good, I can finally go grab some breakfast!" He leaned over and kissed me. "I didn't want to leave until you woke up."

"You don't have to wait on me. Just leave me a note next time."

"I don't feel right about doing that. Besides I would rather give you a kiss when you wake up." He winked and kissed me again. "I'm not going to take anything for granted anymore."

I totally understood because I felt the same way.

After Tom left, Nurse Kelly brought in my breakfast tray. "Guess what, Sherrie? I have great news! The doctor gave the okay to start prepping you for going home. Now, before you get too excited, that doesn't mean you are going home today, but maybe sometime soon if you are able to accomplish certain tasks. Even after you leave, you'll still have a long road to a full recovery with lots of physical therapy. But we know you're a fighter."

After we talked about her news and what would be expected of me, Nurse Kelly asked if we could talk as friends and not nurse to patient. I was surprised because I had befriended most of the nurses, but none had ever requested to talk. I, of course, love a good visit, so I invited her to sit down.

She pulled up a chair next to me and said, "I believe everything you said about Elijah, and I envy you. Not because of the pain you went through because I would never wish that, but I envy the fact that you got to see your son. Both of your sons. You see, I had a miscarriage two years ago. I was five months pregnant with a little girl. I was heartbroken and destroyed for months after losing her. That day you told us about Micah is the day I realized I never named my daughter either. My heart has been broken ever since. So, I wanted to ask you, do you think it's too late to name her?"

"Oh, Kelly, I am so sorry you lost your baby girl. And I don't say those words lightly either. I know you understand that. And, no, I don't think it is too late to give her a name. Ask God for the perfect name, and He will give it to her. In fact, I believe God has already named her, but he will give you her name. It will be fitting and feel as if you have named her yourself."

She wiped her tears and leaned over to hug me. When she sat back in her chair again, she said, "The reason I envy you is because you got to see your kids. So many of us don't. I know you had to go through a lot to get there, but many of us would do so just to get a glimpse of heaven."

Only David and I knew what I was about to tell her. "Kelly, God only sent me back because of a promise. That promise was saving a life. Not my life but another life. You see, God would have let me stay, but I couldn't so a sacrifice had to be made. It was hard, but I knew I didn't have a choice. I had to come back, and now that I am back, I thank the Lord for the gifts He has given me. There are so many gifts that have taken place in my story recently that I can't even believe or conceive. You see, my story could have been a broken story, but because of God, it has become beautiful. Your story, my friend, can be beautiful too. Maybe not in the same aspect as mine but you have your own story to live. Live it well, and don't forget to keep God in it because without Him we would just be broken pieces of a puzzle that are misplaced."

By the time I finished, she was crying pretty hard. We hugged each other again for a long time.

"I need you to know something else, Sherrie. Before you, I never believed in God, but now I want to give my life to God. Will you show me how?"

I explained that all she had to do was pray a simple prayer and then create a relationship with God by continuing to walk with Him. Following Him wouldn't be easy, but after she created that relationship, she would start to hear and feel when He spoke to her. And when He spoke, it was a gift from the Holy Spirit. Then we bowed our heads to pray.

"Jesus, I ask that you forgive me of all of my sins and help me to forgive others as you have forgiven me. I know you gave your life so that I could live and I know you are the Son of God. I ask you this day to come into my life. Lead and guide me in the way I must go and stay with me. Don't ever let me go. In Jesus's name, I pray. Amen."

After the prayer, she hugged me and cleaned up her tears before leaving the room to answer a call from another patient down the hall. She left my room that day a different person, a person with a new life, a gift that only God could give.

CHAPTER 12

FORGIVENESS

After a few more days in the hospital, the time came for me to finally be released. I already knew the road to recovery was going to be long and hard, but I was ready for the new challenge. I was ready to live my life, a different life as Jesus had shown me—the life now available to me.

As Nurse Kelly rolled me down the hall in the wheelchair, I told her how much I appreciated her and all she did. I also told her how elated I was that she was the one to be with me the day I left.

"Well," she said, "I was actually scheduled to be off today, but when I heard you were being released, I asked one of my friends if she would switch shifts with me so I could be here to tell you goodbye. I didn't want to miss this."

I was glad she wanted to share this joyous time with me. She was my absolute favorite nurse, and she was such a blessing to be around.

Before we made it to the elevator, Dr. Gray stepped out of a room and stopped us. "I will truly miss you, Sherrie. And so will others on this floor. I'm very glad I had the opportunity to meet you. I just wish it was under better circumstances. Thank you for sharing your story, and please continue sharing it so others might be saved too."

I told him I would and that I loved helping others see the light. I also thanked him for his care and compassion. He gave me a quick hug and hurried off down the hall.

A few days after my release, we held Elijah's funeral. All of our family and friends attended. It was so hard to say goodbye, but every time I started to cry, I remembered the day I saw Jesus holding our beautiful boy and how mature Elijah already looked and how alert he was. Heaven affects us when we are there, and everything is in sync and perfect. However, I won't lie, Elijah's funeral was the hardest thing I have gone through since the wreck. No pain can compare to losing a child. I always said it wasn't natural for a child to leave the earth before his or her parent. In fact, I had always prayed that if God were to take one of my children, that He would take me too. God answered my prayer and took me, but He also answered David's prayer and returned me.

Now my job is to live life to the fullest and to forgive with all that I have. Sometimes it's hard to forgive, but I know I have to because I don't want to miss out on heaven when it's time for me to leave this earth.

I think the hardest thing I am going through right now is learning to forgive the man who got behind the wheel of that moving truck and drove drunk. Because of him and his sin, my son had to die. Because of him, I have gone through pain I never knew was possible.

I keep telling myself that if he had a harder punishment, I would feel better, but in this case, I don't feel justice prevailed. I do know it's not my place to judge and you do reap what you sow, so he will get his someday. Even if it's not here on earth, God will take care of him.

I was upset when I found out that the judge had sympathy for the driver because he had gone through a divorce, hence the moving truck, and he didn't realize he had drunk as much as he did when he left the house after packing all day. He was sentenced to a few years in jail plus time on probation. But he took a life. This is the part God is working on me about. I have to forgive. Like I said earlier, I am not the judge. God is, and I don't want to be the judge.

Through the struggle of forgiveness, I have learned to pray for Lee, the truck driver, and I have learned that it is not through my strength but the strength of God. I have also learned to ask God to forgive him for me, and in my prayers, release has come and is coming more and more each day that I pray. I just have to be diligent and pray. I know all too well that anger towards someone doesn't hurt that person, but it hurts me. This is why I have to release all anger and unforgiveness. I have to trust God and pray for those who bring hurt into our lives because through that I am released.

It's like my Mom always used to say, "Don't let one person keep you from heaven." That one person could be me, and I don't want to live that life of anger, regret, frustration, or unforgiveness. I want to live a life of freedom. That is why I choose to forgive and release it all over to God, and because of that, I have a gift.

Now, looking back, I see that the gift would have never been given if the promise had never been made. I thank God constantly for the promise made, and because of that promise, my son and I have the gift of new life.

The promise became the gift. Thank you, Lord, for the promise and for the gifts.

HIS PROMISED GIFT

ABOUT THE AUTHOR

Christina (Chris) Stokesbury is a successful business owner. She is author of *Refuse to Stay Broken, Behind the Veil,* and *In Training: Finding the Way.* Chris has worked in a women's prison ministry, taught Sunday school, and lead a Christian home group for many years. She is a faithful Bible reader, devoted wife, and a loving mother to four children, plus one son who is in heaven.

Refuse to Stay Broken
ISBN: 978-1943496037

Christina's memoir talks about the loss of her son Abiah and the healing journey God took her on after Abiah tragically passed away. Through her story, readers will see how God can take what was once bad and turn it into beauty.

Behind the Veil
ISBN: 979-8985807615

Plagued by a fear of the demons she's sensed over the years, Elaina longs to see the good in the world. Join her on her journey and find hope, faith, trust, and a view of life without the veil that separates the seen from the unseen.

In Training: Finding the Way
ISBN: 978-0578437620

This self-help guide focuses on those who feel stuck and out of control when dealing with life's obstacles. The lessons look at issues in life from a positive viewpoint and can foster a new way of understanding life's difficult situations.